Doing Nothing!

Written and illustrated by Petr Horáček

The frog was at the bottom of the pond. Doing nothing!

She climbed on to a rock.

She sat on a rock doing nothing.
Hiss! Look out!

4

The frog had to hop!

Then she sat on a leaf doing nothing.
Miaow! Look out!

The frog had to hop!

Then she sat on the grass doing nothing.
Peck! Look out!

The frog had to hop!

She hopped and hopped and climbed and jumped and ...

SLIP ...

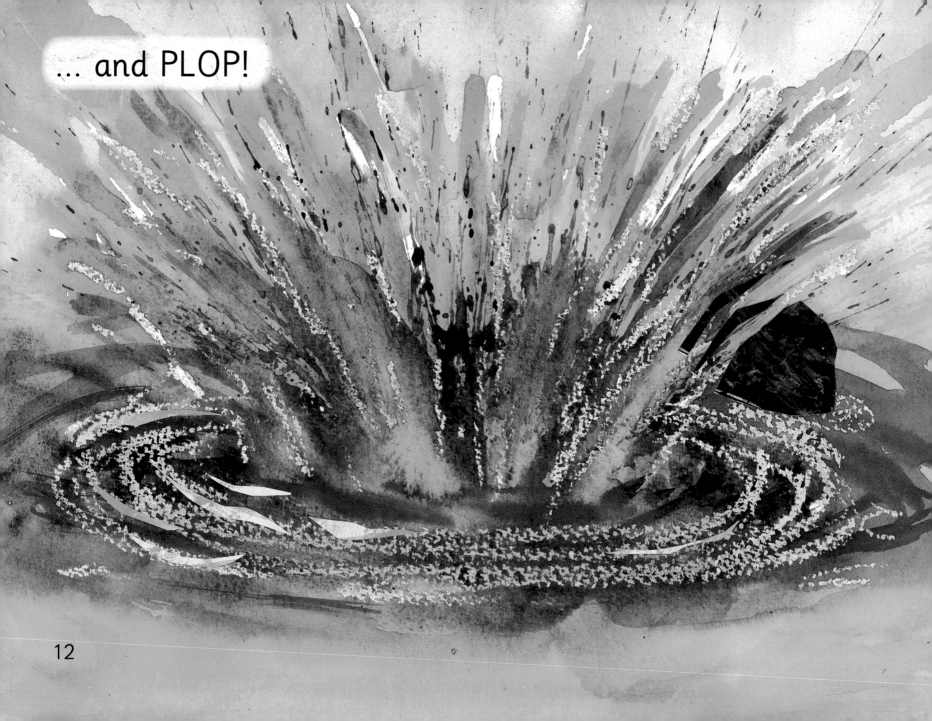

The frog was back at the bottom of the pond.
Doing nothing!

Look out!

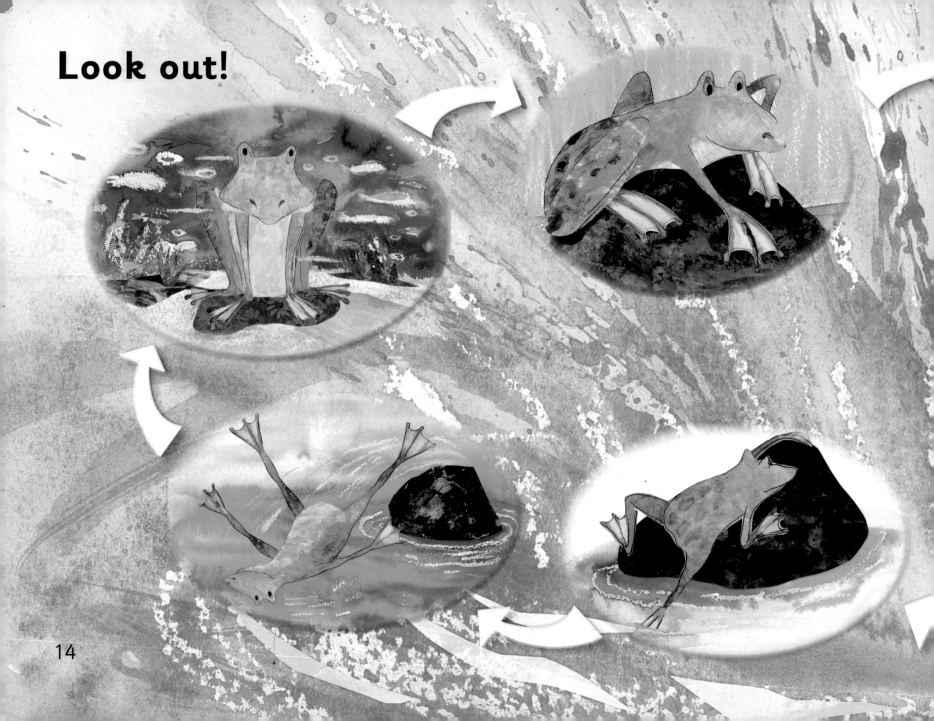

Ideas for reading

Written by Clare Dowdall BA(Ed), MA(Ed)
Lecturer and Primary Literacy Consultant

Learning objectives: read more challenging texts which can be decoded using their acquired phonic knowledge and skills, along with automatic recognition of high frequency words; identify the main events and characters in stories, and find specific information in simple texts; make predictions showing an understanding of ideas, events and characters; ask and answer questions, make relevant contributions, offer suggestions and take turns; retell stories, ordering events using story language

Curriculum links: Science: Plants and animals in the local environment; P.E.: Gymnastic activities

High frequency words: had, then, back

Interest words: bottom, doing, nothing, hiss, miaow, peck, hopped, climbed, jumped

Resources: whiteboard, paper and scissors

Word count: 88

Getting started

- Ask children to tell the group what they know about frogs, e.g. what they do, what they eat, what eats them.

- Look at the word *nothing*. Notice that it is a two syllable word, made up of smaller words, *no-thing*.

- Look at the front and back covers together. Ask the children to read the title and the blurb aloud, and to describe what is happening in the pictures.

- Ask children to share their ideas and to predict what is going to happen in the story.

Reading and responding

- Read pp2–3 together. Discuss the function of the exclamation mark and model expressive reading.

- Look at the word *climbed*. Notice the silent *b* and the *ed* ending. Remind children of the strategies that they can use to attempt longer tricky words, including sounding out, using the context and pictures and using familiar endings.